First published in hardback in Great Britain by Andersen Press Ltd in 1995
First published in paperback by Picture Lions in 1996
New edition published by Collins Picture Books in 2001
This edition published by HarperCollins Children's Books in 2006

5 7 9 10 8 6 4

ISBN 978-0-00-723620-6

Picture Lions and Collins Picture Books are imprints of the Children's Division, part of HarperCollins Publishers Ltd.
HarperCollins Children's Books is a division of HarperCollins Publishers Ltd.

Text and illustrations copyright © Tony Ross 1995, 2001

Visit our website at: www.harpercollins.co.uk

Printed and bound by South China Printing Co.Ltd

I Want My Dinner

Tony Ross

HarperCollins *Children's Books*

"I WANT MY DINNER!"

"Say PLEASE," said the Queen.

"I want my dinner... please."

"Mmmmm, lovely."

"I want my potty."

"Say PLEASE," said the General.

"I want my potty, PLEASE."

"Mmmmm, lovely."

"I want my Teddy...

...PLEASE," said the Princess.

"Mmmmm."

"We want to go for a walk... PLEASE."

"Mmmmm."

"Mmmmm... that looks good."

"HEY!" said the Beastie.

"That's MY dinner."

"I want my dinner!"

"Say PLEASE," said the Princess.

"I want my dinner, PLEASE."

"Mmmmm."

"HEY!" said the Princess.

"Say THANK YOU."

More funny stories featuring the demanding Little Princess!

Tony Ross was born in London in 1938. His dream was to work with horses but instead he went to art college in Liverpool. Since then, Tony has worked as an art director at an advertising agency, a graphic designer, a cartoonist, a teacher and a film maker – as well as illustrating over 250 books! Tony, his wife Zoe and family live in Macclesfield, Cheshire.

I Want My Potty — Tony Ross
978-0-00-723621-3

I Want To Be — Tony Ross
978-0-00-724282-5

I Want My Dinner — Tony Ross
978-0-00-723620-6

I Want My Dummy — Tony Ross
978-0-00-724283-2

I Don't Want To Wash My Hands — Tony Ross
978-0-00-715072-4

I Want My Tooth — Tony Ross
978-0-00-724365-5

I Don't Want To Go To Bed — Tony Ross
978-0-00-725448-4

I Want My Mum — Tony Ross
978-0-00-725449-1

I Want A Friend — Tony Ross
978-0-00-721491-4

"The Little Princess has huge appeal to toddlers and Tony Ross's illustrations are brilliantly witty."
Practical Parenting